anderson & roe
DUOS & DUETS

St. Mat...
Suite...

Johann Sebastian Bach
Arranged by Greg Anderson

Foreword

About the *St. Matthew Passion*

The *St. Matthew Passion* was first performed in 1727 at the St. Thomas Church in Leipzig. Considering it his most significant work, Johann Sebastian Bach revised the passion in 1736 and twice during the early 1740s. Nonetheless, it was shelved after its initial performances and promptly neglected, as was customary for music of the day. The passion received a second premiere of sorts in 1829 when the 19-year-old Felix Mendelssohn organized a performance and conducted the work for the first time since Bach did so himself, albeit in an abbreviated and modified form. The performance was a great success, and this triumphant revival of a historical work did much to establish the modern-day notion of "classical music." Bach's *St. Matthew Passion* has since remained one of the monuments of the literature.

Essentially a form of interactive theater, the *St. Matthew Passion* depicts the final sufferings and crucifixion of Jesus Christ. It sets chapters 26 and 27 of the Gospel of Matthew to music, sung in recitative by the various characters portrayed within the text. This is interspersed with personal reflection on the biblical verse, heard in Bach's recitatives and arias set to a libretto

by Picander, a contemporary of Bach. Mediating between the gospel and its commentary are 15 chorales; these stem from the liturgy and serve as a community response to the unfolding events. The entire production involves a large cast of performers: two choirs, two orchestras, and multiple vocal soloists.

The *St. Matthew Passion* is filled with multidimensional levels of symbolism, theological understanding, and psychological insight. It is undoubtedly one of the most impressive examples of Christian artwork.

About the Arrangement

I wrote this arrangement for two pianos for one simple reason: I wished to play this awe-inspiring music myself. Five movements from the original work have been carefully selected; together they retain the dramatic arch of the story, but pare the music down to a more manageable duration suitable for performance on recitals. The three original arias—one each for solo alto, soprano, and bass, respectively—are in actuality duets of equal partnership between the vocal soloists and obbligato instruments. The counterpoint translates especially well to the two-piano medium. The two chorales in the arrangement serve

Alfred Music Publishing Co., Inc.
P.O. Box 10003
Van Nuys, CA 91410-0003
alfred.com

ISBN-10: 0-7390-9420-3
ISBN-13: 978-0-7390-9420-4

Cover Photo
Bratislava: detail of gothic altar from St. Martin's cathedral, Jesus in Gethsemane garden: © Shutterstock.com / Renata Sedmakova

the same purpose as they do in the original passion: they offer an alternative point of view, both musically and spiritually.

The aria **"Erbarme Dich"** immediately follows a recitative set to Matthew 26:69–75, which recounts Peter's repeated denial of Jesus and his eventual realization of his sins. The aria itself expresses Peter's penitence through the lamenting words of Picander's poem:

> Have mercy,
> My God, for my tears' sake!
> Look hither,
> My heart and eyes weep before you
> Bitterly.

This aria was originally scored as a duet between alto voice and solo violin, accompanied by strings and continuo. Peter's weeping is portrayed through the pervasive use of appoggiaturas, descending bass lines, and piercing dissonances, which in turn prompts us as listeners to take on Peter's repentance as our own.

After Jesus' fate has been decided by an unhinged crowd screaming "Let him be crucified!" the congregation sings the chorale **"Wie wunderbarlich ist doch diese Strafe!"**:

> How amazing is this punishment!
> The good Shepherd suffers for his sheep,
> As righteous as he is, the master pays the penalty
> For his servants.

The chorales would have been as familiar to the original churchgoers as nursery rhymes are to school children, though within the context of the passion, they surely would have carried an intensified meaning. Johann Heermann wrote this particular hymn in 1630 and Johann Crüger wrote its tune 10 years later; the harmonization is by Bach. The chorale is notable for its chromaticism and unusually long musical phrases.

The aria **"Aus Liebe will mein Heiland sterben"** is something of an anomaly in the chaotic midst of Jesus' crucifixion. At once sad, heavenly, and bleakly sparse, the aria underlines one of the central themes of the passion: that Christ died for the love of humankind. Above an ethereal instrumentation of two oboes and a flute, a reflective soprano sings:

> Out of love,
> Out of love my Savior is willing to die,
> Though he knows nothing of any sin,
> So that eternal ruin
> And the punishment of judgment
> May not rest upon my soul.

Bach omits the usual strings and continuo to symbolize Christ's otherworldly purity.

The chorale **"O Haupt voll Blut und Wunden"** represents a low point of sorts, both in its uncompromising imagery and in its placement within the narrative.

> O head, full of blood and wounds,
> Full of sorrow and full of scorn,
> O head, bound in mockery
> With a crown of thorns,
> O head, once beautifully adorned
> With highest honor and renown,
> But now shamefully mistreated,
> Let me hail thee!

The text and melody to this chorale have a tangled past that illustrates the free flow of artistic ideas throughout history. The hymn is based on a medieval Latin poem and was translated into German by the Lutheran hymnist Paul Gerhardt in the mid-seventeenth century. The melody is by Hans Leo Hassler, written around 1600 for a secular love song and later simplified by Johann Crüger to accompany Gerhardt's hymn. Bach, once again, re-harmonized the chorale for its use in his passion. Ironically, the melody of Paul Simon's "American Tune" is also based on the same German melody.

Passions are typically performed on Good Friday, and, as such, they do not depict Jesus' resurrection. Even so, a certain resolution is attained near the conclusion of Bach's *St. Matthew Passion*. During the recitative preceding **"Mache dich, mein Herze, rein,"** the bass proclaims, *"Peace is now made with God, for Jesus has endured his cross. His body comes to rest."* Then, along with the strings, continuo, and a pair of oboes, the bass sings an aria that demonstrates how far we've come as participants in the story:

> *Make yourself pure, my heart,*
> *For I will bury Jesus within me,*
> *For now within me, he shall*
> *For ever and ever*
> *Take his sweet rest.*
> *World, leave my heart, and let Jesus enter!*

No longer anguished by Jesus' suffering, we enter a state of mind wholly new, serene, and quietly euphoric. Salvation is indeed at hand.

In conclusion, the structure of both the *St. Matthew Passion* and this arrangement follow Martin Luther's "A Meditation on Christ's Passion," written in 1519. Luther first asks the believer to repent his own guilt and show remorse ("Erbarme Dich"), then recognize that Christ suffered for our sins (the chorales) and that his love will conquer all ("Aus Liebe will mein Heiland sterben"). Having undertaken these earlier stages, the believer can finally accept Christ into his life and live following Christ's example ("Mache dich, mein Herze, rein").

Audiences of this arrangement, however, are free to give the work new meaning. With simplified instrumentation and no lyrics at hand, the music becomes abstract, reduced to its purest essence. The pianos' monochromatic sonority and clarity of attack highlight the harmonic complexities within the music; the tormented dissonances become even more tangible. Words are no longer necessary: the music speaks for itself, with poignancy and intensity.

Regardless of one's religious beliefs, the *St. Matthew Passion* is a work of haunting beauty and emotional power, a work capable of inspiring self-reflection and personal growth. Though ostensibly about one man's death, it is music that gives us a reason to live.

Performance Suggestions

Dynamics: Bach himself included very few dynamic markings in the score. The process of arranging thusly gives me a significant voice in the interpretation of the work; the decisions I made regarding density, texture, and register greatly affect the music's structure and momentum. Be that as it may, the dynamics listed are still merely suggestions. In the end, the subtleties of performance—volume, character, tonal color, and structural emphasis—are up to the performers. Conviction of interpretation is vastly preferred to dogmatic adherence to the score.

Articulations and ornaments: For the most part, I followed Bach's original articulations closely. Ornaments should be played on the beat in order to maximize the potency of the dissonances. In general, the symbol *tr* refers to melodic trills that extend throughout the duration of the note; the ♦♦ symbols refer to trills that are played in a more ornamental manner and should contain only a few turns. Pianists should play all two-note slurs with great care and nuance; they account for much of the music's soul.

Tempos: The tempo indications and metronome markings offer only a guidepost for performers. Elizabeth Joy Roe and I perform the music with great freedom. Some pianists may even choose to consider unusual tempi, as there are no restrictions related to breath support.

Acknowledgments

I am deeply grateful to my piano duo partner and friend, Elizabeth Joy Roe, without whom this arrangement would not exist. I offer my effusive thanks for her assistance in all matters of this publication, from her editorial and musical suggestions to her help with this foreword. Her insight, encouragement, and supreme musicality know no bounds.

Additional thanks go to Julian Martin whose editorial assistance has enormously benefited the arrangement of "Erbarme Dich."

—Greg Anderson

St. Matthew Passion
Suite for Two Pianos

Johann Sebastian Bach (1685–1750)
BWV 244
Arr. Greg Anderson

ⓐ Play the ornaments on the beat unless otherwise indicated.

ⓑ In passages of melodic octaves, the lower notes should be played very quietly, like a shadow.

Chorale: Wie wunderbarlich ist doch diese Strafe!

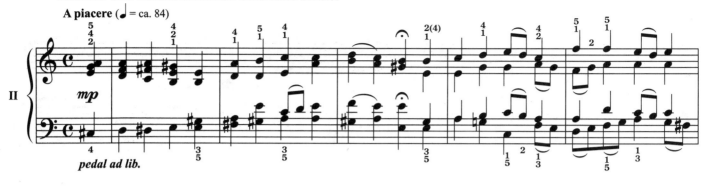

Aria: Aus Liebe will mein Heiland sterben

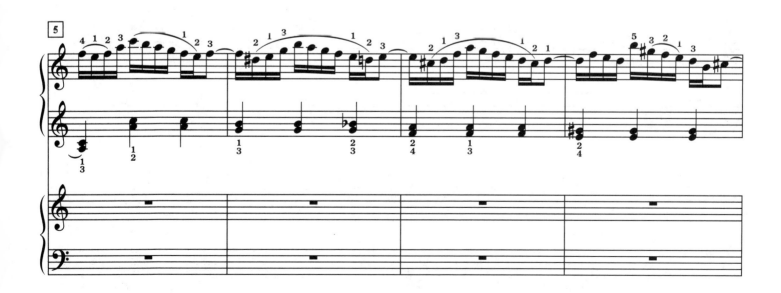

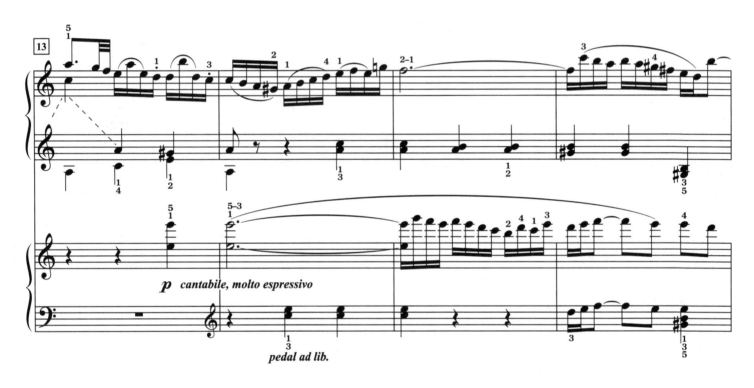

p cantabile, molto espressivo

pedal ad lib.

Chorale: O Haupt voll Blut und Wunden

Aria: Mache dich, mein Herze, rein